The Knightly Campout

adapted by Cordelia Evans
based on the screenplay written by Simon Nicholson

Ready-to-Read

Simon Spotlight
New York   London   Toronto   Sydney   New Delhi

SIMON SPOTLIGHT
An imprint of Simon & Schuster Children's Publishing Division
1230 Avenue of the Americas, New York, New York 10020
For information about special discounts for bulk purchases, please contact Simon & Schuster Special Sales at 1-866-506-1949 or business@simonandschuster.com.
Manufactured in the United States of America 0414 LAK
First Edition 10 9 8 7 6 5 4 3 2 1
ISBN 978-1-4814-0418-1 (pbk)
ISBN 978-1-4814-0419-8 (hc)
ISBN 978-1-4814-0420-4 (eBook)

Sparkie and Squirt were

taking a nap.

Mike decided he wanted

to do something knightly.

Their nap gave him an idea!

Mike woke up the dragons.

"I want to camp overnight

in the Tall Tree Woods!"

he said.

Mike hopped on Galahad.
He reached for his sword
and pulled out a cup of . . .

"Hot chocolate?" asked

Sparkie.

"I will not need that on my

campout," said Mike.

Squirt had a list of things
that Mike would need.
But Mike said he was going
to camp with nothing.
That was the knightly way!

Mike tried to build

a tent out of sticks.

But it fell down.

Finally, he got it to stay.

Then he saw that Sparkie and Squirt had a big tent to sleep in.

Mike gathered more sticks
to make a bed.

It was not comfy.

Squirt got out his bed.

It was very comfy!

"Do you want a blanket,

Mike?" asked Squirt.

"No, thank you," said Mike. "I am camping out the knightly way."

Then the dragons made
campout stew.

"Mike, we have some stew
for you!" said Squirt.

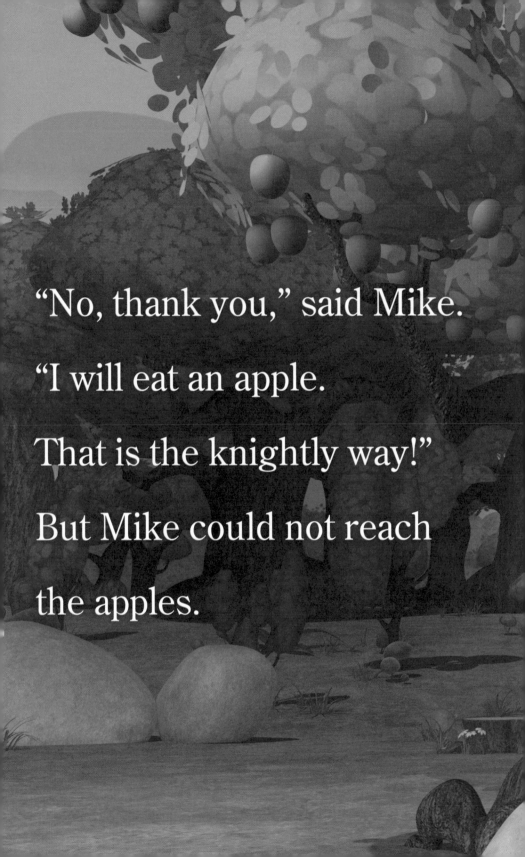

"No, thank you," said Mike.

"I will eat an apple.

That is the knightly way!"

But Mike could not reach

the apples.

"Here is a box to stand on!" said Squirt.

"Here is a ladder!" said Sparkie.

"No, thank you," said Mike.

"Oh no!" said Mike. "I wanted to do things the knightly way, with no help!"

"It is okay if we help,"

said Sparkie.

"As long as you sleep outside all night, you are still knightly!"

"I guess you are right," said Mike.

The dragons helped Mike fix his tent and gave him stew.

Mike shared his hot
chocolate.

Then they all went to bed.

They slept outside all night.

It was the perfect knightly

campout!